W9-AYF-442

FRANK ASCH

The Earth and I

Voyager Books • Harcourt, Inc.
Orlando Austin New York San Diego London

Copyright © 1994 by Frank Asch

All rights reserved. No part of this publication may be reproduced or transmitted in any form or by any means, electronic or mechanical, including photocopy, recording, or any information storage and retrieval system, without permission in writing from the publisher.

Requests for permission to make copies of any part of the work should be submitted online at www.harcourt.com/contact or mailed to the following address: Permissions Department, Harcourt, Inc., 6277 Sea Harbor Drive, Orlando, Florida 32887-6777.

www.HarcourtBooks.com

First Voyager Books edition 2008

Voyager Books is a trademark of Harcourt, Inc., registered in the United States of America and/or other jurisdictions.

The Library of Congress has cataloged the hardcover edition as follows:
Asch, Frank.
The earth and I/Frank Asch.
p. cm.
Summary: A child explains how he and the Earth dance and sing together and take turns listening to each other.
[1. Earth—Fiction.] I. Title.
PZ7.A778Ear 1994
E—dc20 93-237
ISBN 978-0-15-200443-9
ISBN 978-0-15-206395-5 pb

TWP 11 10 9 8 7 6
4500268672

The paintings in this book were done in watercolors, acrylics, and colored pencils on Arches watercolor paper, series 500.
The display type was set in Billy.
The text type was set in Columbus.
Color separations by Bright Arts, Ltd., Singapore
Printed and bound by Tien Wah Press, Singapore
Production supervision by Christine Witnik
Designed by Trina Stahl and Lori J. McThomas

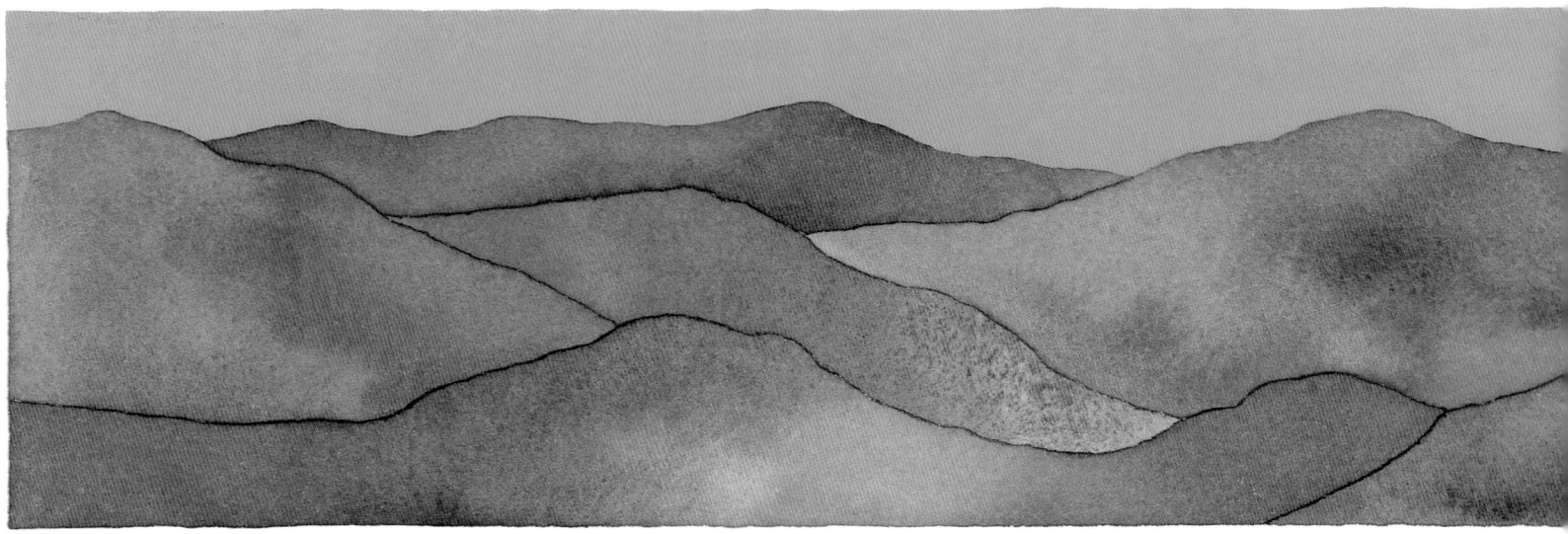

for Lynne and Eric

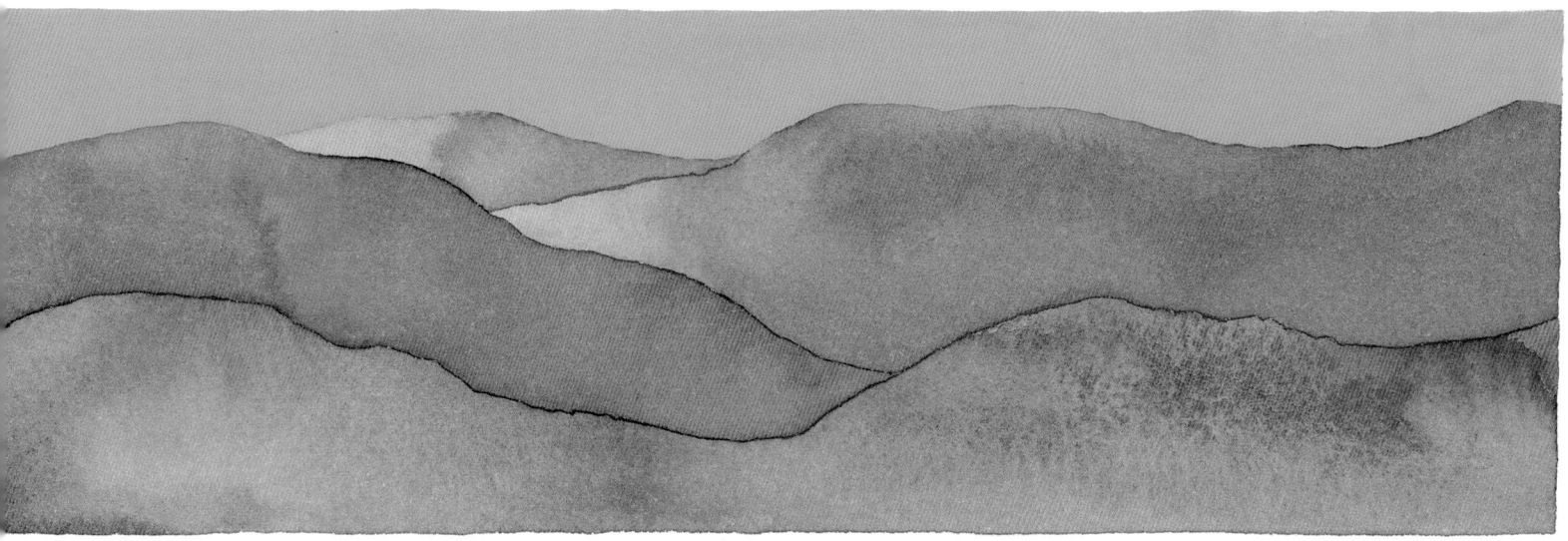

The Earth and I are friends.

Sometimes we go for long walks together.

I tell her what's on my mind.

She listens to every word.

Then I listen to her.

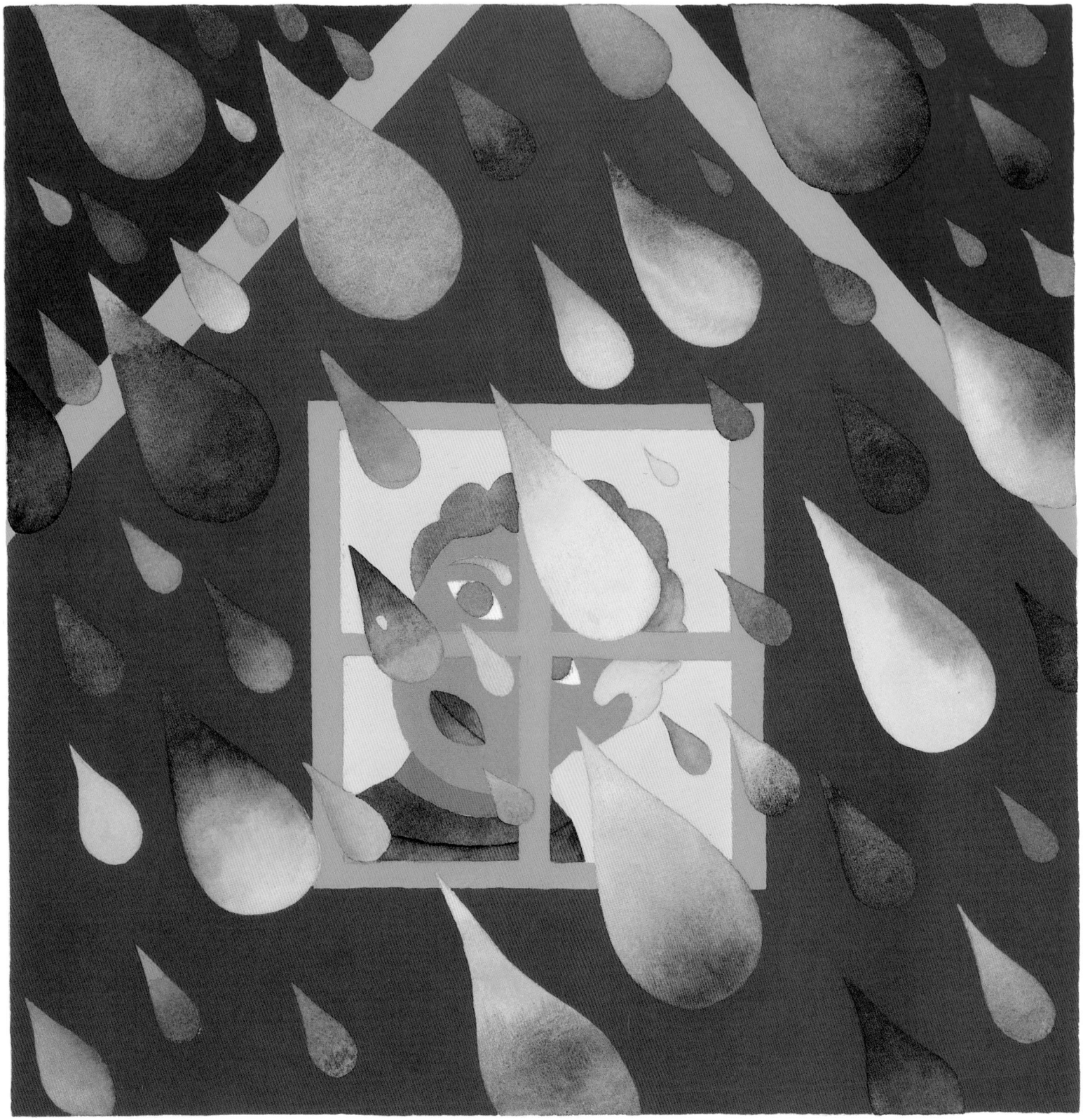

The Earth and I are friends.

We play together in my backyard.

I help her to grow.

She helps me to grow.

I sing for her.

She sings for me.

I dance for her.

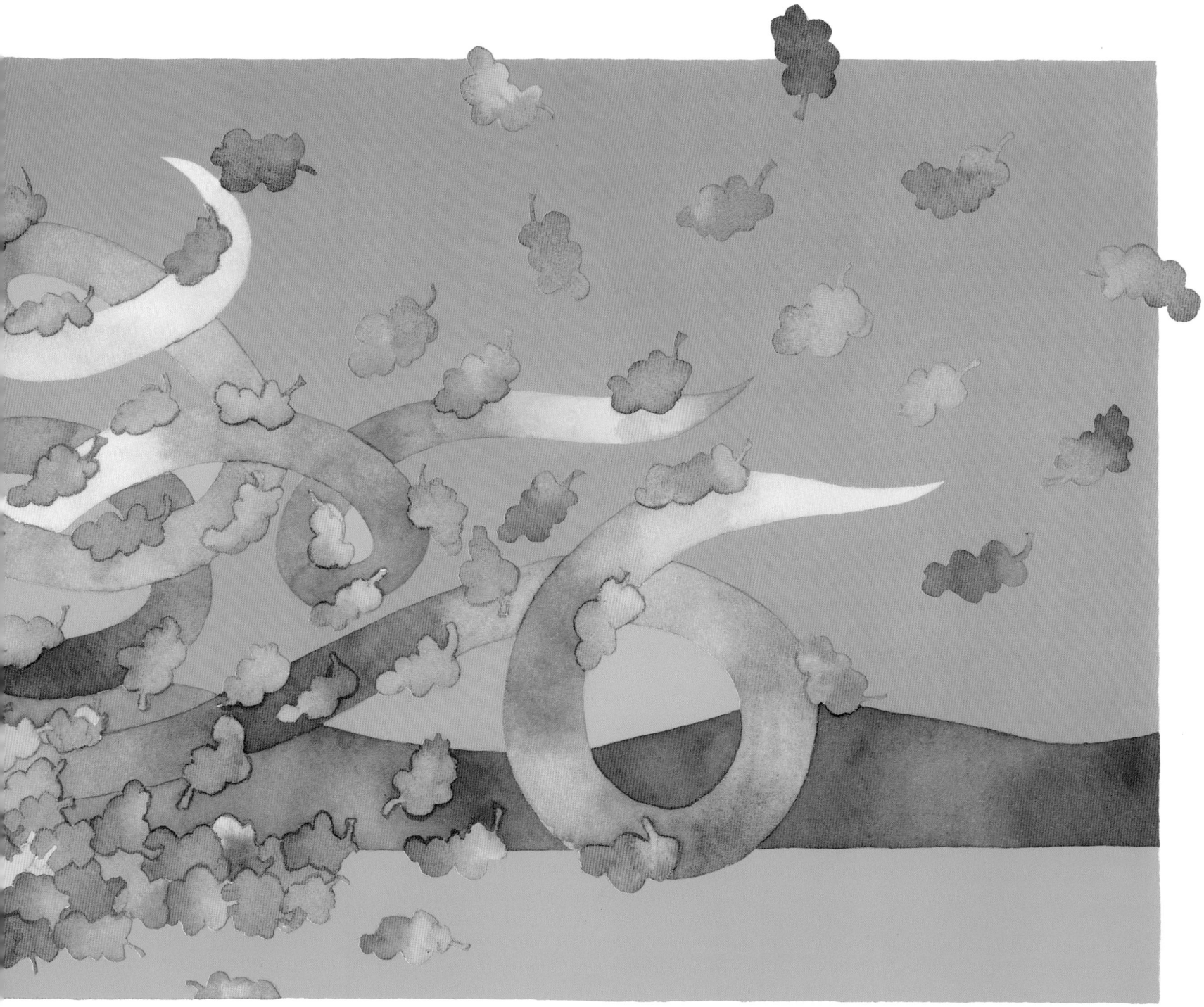

She dances for me.

When she's sad,

I'm sad.

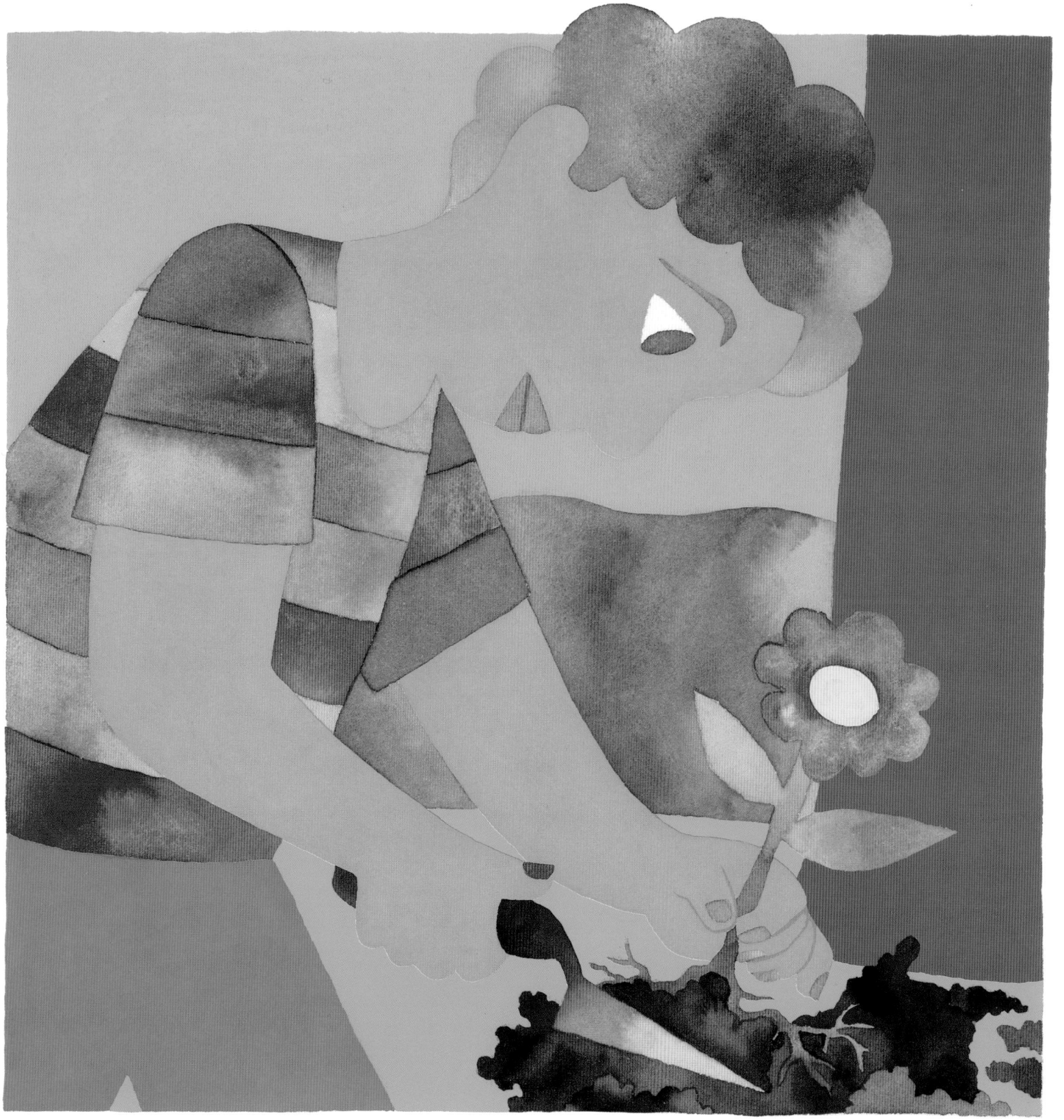

When she's happy,

I'm happy.

The Earth and I are friends.